This book belongs to

_____

_____

To Marcus, Marie-Hélène, Rowan and River. Happy Christmas!
C. C.

To my own patient elf.
J. P.

Faber has published children's books since 1929. T. S. Eliot's *Old Possum's Book of Practical Cats* and Ted Hughes' *The Iron Man* were amongst the first. Our catalogue at the time said that 'it is by reading such books that children learn the difference between the shoddy and the genuine'. We still believe in the power of reading to transform children's lives. All our books are chosen with the express intention of growing a love of reading, a thirst for knowledge and to cultivate empathy. We pride ourselves on responsible editing. Last but not least, we believe in kind and inclusive books in which all children feel represented and important.

First published in the UK in 2021
First published in the US in 2021
by Faber and Faber Limited
Bloomsbury House,
74–77 Great Russell Street,
London WC1B 3DA

Text © Caroline Crowe, 2021
Illustrations © Jess Pauwels, 2021
Designed by Faber and Faber
HB ISBN 978–0–571–36447–3
PB ISBN 978–0–571–36448–0

Printed in India
10 9 8 7 6 5 4 3 2 1
The moral rights of Caroline Crowe and Jess Pauwels have been asserted
A CIP record for this book is available from the British Library

Santa's New Sleigh

Caroline Crowe 🌿 Jess Pauwels

faber

Christmas Eve was here at last.
The countdown clock was ticking fast.
The sleigh was polished, reindeer fed,
And all the children safe in bed.

Starlight lit the inky sky
As elves lined up to wave goodbye.

But yikes! When Santa turned the key,
(The reindeer need some help, you see)
The engine didn't start – it spluttered.
"That isn't right," the elves all muttered.

The garage team all rallied round.
The faulty engine bit was found.
They tried to order in a spare,
But couldn't find one anywhere.

"We have no sleigh! What will we do?"
Poor Santa was in quite a stew.

But elves don't give up in a hurry.
"We'll get those presents out – don't worry!

"Something fast – that's what we need.

How quick can elves run at top speed?"
Not quick enough, with legs that short,
Although it was a helpful thought.

"The post office might find a way?"
No, it was past last posting day.

Skis seemed like a good idea,
But it was very hard to steer.

"A slingshot set up in the trees
Will make delivery a **breeze!**"

But when they tried, one little elf
Hung on too tight and sent himself!

Owls kept dropping from the sky.
They couldn't carry toys and fly,

They tried balloons, but had to stop.
The icicles just made them POP.

And several elves fell off the stairs
They used to climb the polar bears.

The team had tried their very best.
They had to stop and have a rest,
And as they ate a quick mince pie,
The minutes kept on ticking by.

But one small elf was very busy ...

Santa's Head Inventor, Lizzie.
She tightened nuts, banged nails in too,
And other things inventors do,
Till finally she gave a shout,

"I need some help to push this out!"

Santa gasped, the elves all cheered
As something marvellous appeared.

"We'll use this new electric sleigh
I'd started building anyway."

Ho-ray for Lizzie's green solution –
Heated seats and no pollution!
"It needs a charge. Come on elves, quick …

"Cycle power should do the trick!"
Those little legs all pedalled fast.
The battery light pinged on at last.

The giant, bulging present sack
Was safely hoisted in the back.
Santa set the dial to GO.
"You've all saved Christmas. Ho ho ho!"

So now you know why you can't hear
When Santa's sleigh flies very near.

Electric engines make no noise,
And don't wake sleeping girls and boys.

Now Mrs Claus trains elves all year,
With Santa bringing up the rear.

So when it comes to Christmas night,
Elf power keeps the sleigh in flight,

And if the battery light goes dim,
They take a break and plug it in.

Of course, for added festive fun,
New cycling shorts for everyone!